BOA
EDITIONS
LIMITED

THESE UPRAISED HANDS

Poems by

WILLIAM B. PATRICK

BOA Editions, Ltd. ❧ Brockport, NY ❧ 1995

LC #: 95–77861
ISBN: 1–880238–26–8 cloth
ISBN: 1–880238–27–6 paper

First Edition
95 96 97 98   7 6 5 4 3 2 1

Publications by BOA Editions, Ltd.—
a not-for-profit corporation under section 501 (c) (3)
of the United States Internal Revenue Code—
are made possible with the assistance of grants from
the Literature Program of the New York State Council on the Arts,
the Literature Program of the National Endowment for the Arts,
the Lannan Foundation,
as well as from the Rochester Area Foundation Community Arts Fund
administered by the Arts & Cultural Council for Greater Rochester,
the County of Monroe, NY,
and from many individual supporters.

Cover Art: *Slave Ship (Slavers Throwing Overboard the Dead and Dying,
Typhoon Coming On)*, by J. M. W. Turner,
Henry Lillie Pierce Fund,
Courtesy, Museum of Fine Arts, Boston
Cover Design: Daphne Poulin-Stofer
Typesetting: Richard Foerster
Manufacturing: McNaughton & Gunn, Lithographers
BOA Logo: Mirko

Excerpt from *Sex, Art and American Culture*, by Camille Paglia,
copyright © 1992 by Camille Paglia, is used by permission
of Random House, Inc.

BOA Editions, Ltd.
A. Poulin, Jr., President
92 Park Avenue
Brockport, NY 14420

for my sons
Tarin and Caleb

CONTENTS

1

2

3

1

i heard someone singing
i didn't know it was me
i usually sing dreams when i'm not asleep

—Caleb Patrick

AN ACCIDENT

I wish I could make this not true — this story
of what happened fourteen years ago today.

My father owned a thoroughbred horse farm then,
fifty acres of low mountain valley

that he had bulldozed and fenced and paddocked off.
He backhoed the trenches for lines and pipes,

set each locust post, laid his hand on every rail.
I had my own land and house half an hour away.

Once a week I'd drive over to help him out,
for pay, but for time to work beside him, too.

Building his dream-farm wasn't breeding horses, though,
and being a city boy who'd made good

enough to buy some fillies that won, now and then,
just got him inside the right stable of friends.

A splay-footed gelding, a calf-kneed mare —
he couldn't tell how to avoid what at first,

so he found a farm manager who could.
Warren Rodman, back East from Arizona,

could peel a horse's skin off with one steady look,
survey its bone mechanics with X-ray eyes —

point of shoulder to knee, angle of fetlock to hoof.
He called the barn his Palace of Flies.

"If I die right now, I'll leave happy," he'd say.
"I've spent my days living most folks' dreams."

Three years in, they'd logged 20 standing foals,
and every stall in the palace was filled.

The accident day was a Sunday, just like today,
with hard rain that made me wish I'd slept in.

Warren had the tractor in the top paddock, alone,
working the post-hole auger with the power take-off.

Post-holes wanted two pairs of hands, I knew that,
one to keep the running tractor steady

and one to hold the auger arm straight.
My father and his wife were down to Albany.

I couldn't work the tractors there. They worried
about insurance. I wasn't a real employee.

So I set my stance wide to stand in the mud
and pulled down on the metal arm as the auger spun

and caught, slowed then, and bounced as if on rock —
bounced until I pried out a broad stone. Then it caught

and churned plain dirt down to past three feet,
when it found another and took to bouncing again.

I worked the point to what edges I could reach,
but the hole was deep and this stone too broad.

Warren climbed down, laughing, not to be mean
or show he was stronger. We both knew he was.

I'd seen him keep a stallion still with one hand.
He climbed down to help me get the job done.

We moved to one side and rocked the auger arm back
until the take-off bolt spun too close to see.

He was laughing still, and I could never tell
if he was serious or horsing around —

it was all the same for him. Then I heard him yell,
and saw his denim coat was caught on the bolt.

He braced his arms straight. He dug his heels in.
"Shut the tractor off," he shouted to me,

and I ran to it, but I couldn't find the key.
So I jammed every lever its opposite way,

and still it churned along. I ran back to him then,
and grabbed his waist. The take-off bar spun

against my knuckles and carried away the skin.
The mud wouldn't hold. We were both slipping under

when the bolt ate its way through his clothes.
There are some faces or words you can never lose.

His scream in that second ended up caught inside me.
Sorry. You need to see what was happening.

Between the auger arm and the take-off shaft
that a tractor spins to work an auger,

there's a narrow space, the size, I'd guess,
of a newborn baby — maybe a foot and a half.

Warren got pulled through that space twice
and then thrown on his back underneath.

I was jackknifed back when he started through,
landed wrong on my left ankle. Shattered it.

I could hear his coat and shirt flapping, louder
than the tractor engine, until they wrapped tight

and got quiet. Warren, half-bare, didn't move.
I covered him with my shirt and crawled to a phone.

My father's farm was on Fly Summit Road,
and we waited there an hour for a rescue squad.

"We been trying to find you," they said. "A maze of back roads."
They were right. It *is*. All of what I tell you is true.

Warren couldn't speak, but he did cough once,
and a steady, red line bubbled out and stayed.

I kept myself busy wiping it away.
I was crying, which I couldn't do much back then,

and saying I was sorry, over and over.
I know I told him, "Hang on. They'll be here soon."

No bones stuck out. The only part he could move
were his eyes, and he forgave me with them.

After a while, the tractor used up its gas,
and I could hear the rain dance on the mud.

I thought my father would come back again.
Then I remembered when I was seven

he would wake me in the dark for hockey, to play
Pee Wee Hockey. Us little guys played early,

6 or 6:30, and he made hot chocolate,
and he started the car to make it warm,

and I waited in our kitchen with the dark outside
until he hurried back in again for me.

When my father drove in after lunch, we were gone.
A neighbor had tacked a note up on his door.

That night he brought me over to Warren's house,
so I could tell his wife and kids how he died.

"Warren was my mentor. My, my, my . . . friend,"
was what my father said. And wouldn't look at me.

He waited in the car, keeping it warm, I guess.
I angled my crutches up the stairs, knocked, and went in.

My father is still alive. Sometimes I see him.
I could read him this poem, and he'd try to listen.

But he'd probably think, *What can a poem change?*
and those words would appear in a translucent red

across Warren's chest as he floated, smiling,
waving to me, through my father's eyes.

DREAMS WHEN WE'RE NOT ASLEEP

for Tarin

The small boy isn't thinking
of the Yellow Room mat he is supposed to rest on,
or of his tears,
or of his split-open house that hangs above him
on the wall:
a red house with a red chimney
tossing out a jagged bundle of smoke
into an empty sky —
a red house whose yellow roof
the small boy colored partway open earlier today,
tipping it up on one triangular edge
just far enough
for a doctor to check its throat.
The Orange Room is lining up for lunch now.
"Jason, no pushing . . . Jason, TIME OUT."
The teacher's words ricochet up the stairs,
but the small boy is listening now to the wind
on his father's hillside in Vermont.
He can see his father down below,
through the yellow beech leaves and the maples' red,
loading firewood near the run-off stream-bed.
The shagbark hickories are creaking again,
trying to scare him,
rubbing their high branches together,
so with his thumb and first finger
he snaps them apart.
That was easy, the small boy calls down,
and his father waves up at him.
I can change my dreams.
He remembers the white coy-dogs

that killed Allan's sheep,
how both lay in the wide meadow
past his father's woodshop
for half a hot, end-of-August afternoon,
licking the red
off each other's paws and noses and --
Look, Dad, they must be kissing, he'd said then,
but his father told him the truth.
Where are those two?
When he finds them again,
sleeping near the new monastery,
he grabs a chunk of cloud and puzzles out
four flappable wings,
the fat curves quieting out to perfect points.
Here you go, he says,
holding them still to slide each wing into place.
And the coy-dogs disappear along a ladder of sunlight.
Anything can happen in my dreams, he thinks,
but right away his hard memories start to line up,
palms out,
waiting to be changed:
the loud bees in the blighted elm;
his new, orange snow tube
tipping toward the culvert's sharp lip;
the black snake sticking its tongue out
underneath the old freezer;
his father sitting on the boy's bed, crying, explaining,
"There are more people in Boston";
his father standing in the long kitchen window,
waving as the packed car hurries
around the hill;
his mother turning up the car radio
as the boy makes his bear
wave back.
The boy doesn't want any of these.

He sees the two-foot food pile he made
that last morning in Vermont,
all one cupboard's insides propped against the back door,
and he begins again:
Start with a round box of salt,
then add a brand new bottle of black sauce
that won't wash out of your clothes.
He sees his mother's car coming back around the hill.
One heavy bag of King Arthur's white flour — dropped.
Crystallized clover honey,
seventeen wooden spoonfuls.
His father turns toward him from the window.
White rice, brown rice, noodle elbows, spaghetti sticks,
as much as you have,
all mixed in.
His mother throws her bags down in the upstairs hallway.
Half a bottle of olive oil, extra pressed,
shaken empty,
and barbecue sauce, squeezed until air comes out.
The boy hears clapping behind him, and he speeds up.
Shake Italian bread crumbs in circles,
from the outside in.
Pour on diagonal lines of cinnamon and oregano.
Sprinkle sweet coconut from as high as —
His parents are sitting together now,
banging their knives and forks on the glass table,
impatient for this breakfast.
The boy laughs.
His father taught him how to cook.
He knows how to finish off a masterpiece.
He lifts the one bag left,
the white one with a red house and yellow letters.
Old fashioned buckwheat pancake mix,
one whole bag, he sings out.
Get your taste-buds ready, Mom,

it's almost done.
I told you, Dad, this is easy.
You two just sit together and kiss.
I'll mix in the warm water and stir it up.
You just add water.
It's easy.

LOVE POEM ON THE ROAD TO MEMPHIS

for Stacey

When the Mecklenburg prison bus slowed
and turned left,
I saw one dark hand
stretch its fingers down
between the horizontal window-bars
and signal back toward me,
twice before I passed,
the way an amputee might dream of waving
to an old friend.
A skunk's warning blanketed the reservoir bridge,
and a mottled calf strained,
splay-legged,
craning its isosceles head
for a fresh place to suck.
Against the red, combed hilltop,
a line of plastic quonset huts —
three pellucid flower-houses —
filtered a moment
of perfect, horizontal sunlight
and shamed the mockingbirds
into a reverent silence
that puzzled them,
just as once in Vermont's Northeast Kingdom
I rounded a steep curve at sunset
and faced a lake-sized pond
covered shore to shore
with opalescent
water-lilies.

If I could build either moment's quiet shock
into one divine word,
I could carry it back for you —
I who keep offering up words.

KINDERGARTEN DAY

You'll be the first one on the bus,
the first kid it stops for.
You get to pick the best seat,
right up in front near the driver.
It goes to kindergarten, remember?
We went there last week,
after we unpacked from Virginia.
Yes, there are still fleeches in our swamp there.
And it's not fleech.
It starts with an "l", like lost,
no, like lemonade.
You'll be the only kid on the bus for one turn,
but it's a quick one,
right past those short pine trees.
I don't know if there are more ants than pine trees
in the whole world.
What do you think?
Of course we'll wave.
We'll wave until you're all the way past the trees.
No, I promise,
the bus goes to your school,
the long building with the red swings outside,
next to the Black Angus field,
with all the cows that don't give milk,
next to the blue water tower,
remember?
You said it was the spaceship
that brought you here from Out West.
I know you're not kidding.
I believe you.
No, that's not a gulture.

It's a crow.
And it's not gulture,
It starts with a "v", like video.
Crows don't eat people.
I don't know if you watch cartoons in kindergarten.
Your teacher's name is Mrs. Klose.
You won't get lost.
They write your name on a paper card
and stick it on your shirt,
C-A-L-E-B, Caleb,
big enough so everyone can see it,
so on the first day they'll know where you belong.
No, Mrs. Klose won't squeeze you to death
if you talk in kindergarten.
I promise.
Who told you that?
Emily goes to a different school.
It isn't true.
Here comes the bus.
Remember,
one chocolate milk for snack.
The quarter's in your pocket, right here.
Your sandwich is in your new pack.
Yes, you have to eat the lettuce
and all the carrot sticks before your cookies.
Your thermos unscrews to the left.
No, this is your left.
Sherry is your bus driver.
Yes, you can talk to her.
She's not that kind of stranger.
Of course we love you.
Smoke, I know.
You're right, that's pollution.
Tell Mrs. Klose about it.
The bus isn't going Out West.

Yes, the house will still be here after school.
Okay, it's not called school.
It's kindergarten.
Yes, Mom and I will be here.
Go ahead now.
Remember,
wave until you pass the pines.
We'll stand right here.
Yes.
When you come home.
Yes.
Good-bye.
Don't forget to keep waving.
Yes, we'll still see you.
The bus windows aren't that dirty.
Yes.
Have fun.
Good-bye.
Yes.

THE TELEPHONE

rings
and you answer it
No one answers you
and so you hang up
You check your watch
eleven forty-five at night seems late
too late for someone
casing your house
anyone who cares if you're home
If it were nine-thirty on a Tuesday morning
well that would be different
wouldn't it
It rings again
but you hear the same dead air as before
Now you remember that your wife has been out
with Vic and Elizabeth
at a new movie
a romantic comedy
she said
but she left at five-thirty
and the multiplex doesn't show double features
So okay
they went to eat somewhere
it's not even that late
unless there's been
what
an accident
or a spontaneous opportunity
worse yet an entirely pre-planned evening
maybe it wasn't Vic and Elizabeth
after all

maybe she's hurrying off to Memphis
curled against some black-haired preacher
whose big free foot pumps in time
to new Christian rock
on his Taurus CD player
Then you remember
she invited four of your colleagues for dinner
tomorrow night
and she spent all afternoon shopping
then tasting her special olive-caper marinade
for the eight defrosting chicken breasts in the sink
Why would she set all that up
just so she
The ringing starts again
but this time
after you let all four rings
echo through the empty kitchen
you hear your own voice say you're not here
say please leave a message
and then you monitor more dead air
This happened once before
twenty years ago
when you lived near Syracuse
in the white Catholic church you bought and re-habbed
you and your first wife
whose mother is dying of cancer
right now
as you stand there waiting for another call
with a hole spreading in your L. L. Bean slippers
the pair she gave you that final Vermont Christmas
the one before she took your son
to live in Boston
the one who called yesterday
to say his grandmother is really dying this time

so you know
and she knows you know
You're the last person
your first wife would call if she's in pain
But in that de-sanctified church
your first year past graduate school
sleeping in the loft you built above the altar
the phone would ring late
night after night
sometimes for weeks straight
even after you changed the number
and no one ever answered you then either
The locals prayed you'd leave
because they all got married in that old church
for god's sake
You don't do it in there do you they wondered aloud
their confirmation names
swimming up into their stares
But maybe it wasn't them at all
Maybe it was the car salesman
whose name you have forgotten now
the one who sold you the church
the one who raped his daughters next door
until his drunk wife fell off the porch
one final time
and hollered all along our main street
she'd had enough
she didn't care who knew anymore
The calls stopped as soon as he left town
didn't they
It rings again
Pick it up and talk for a while
Maybe one of your father's four bypassed arteries has
what

clogged malfunctioned burst
propelled a thoughtless hunk of plaque toward his brain
wait a minute
they're bypassed
and his wife would call for him when it was over
wouldn't she
Still anything can happen
especially these days
He could be for whatever reason alone
dialing in delusion your number
which is seven hundred miles away
and he just can't talk
Or maybe your brother who lives at Riley House
and collects ballpoint pens
has fallen in the bathroom during a shift change
and grief has injected a temporary amnesia
into your mother's vocal cords
Or maybe she is having a stroke
Hello
Who is this
What do you want
How long are you going to do this
It's past midnight you know
One more time
and I alert the operator to what you're doing okay
Nothing
no calculated breath
no threat
no hushed whispering in the background
no muffled laughter
no pause no click no final dialtone
you could get lost in
like an electronic ocean of remembered conversations
creeping up and up

toward your ragged line of picked-over shells
caught in sea-trash
But it is ringing again now
Listen
Somebody wants you

TEETH

Seven days before Christmas,
1965,
Charlie Morrison,
our tight-lipped, hate-eyed, Canadian hockey coach,
blew his whistle twice,
and the two of us skated out,
me and Freddie Plunkett
from our opposite corners,
rushing toward the center face-off circle,
half a rink away.
From the other corners, players fired passes,
so if somehow you could watch
from up above,
if, say, we had been important enough
to mount a television camera up there,
or if you could lie suspended
from the curved, white-enamelled girders
that gave the grey roof its apex,
you could watch a recurring flux of motion below,
skaters and pucks crisscrossing,
forming a perilous split-second where each had to sense
the other player's path —
and gauge how near he was
when you looked away to catch your pass.
"Man on the left side,"
Charlie Morrison could have yelled,
or, since he had to include some danger,
"Heads up when you hear his skates glide,"
but Charlie wouldn't talk to us much.
And he never spoke if we were losing.
I can't remember,

that day a week from Christmas,
what went wrong,
but my front teeth ended up in Freddie's forehead.

I was 16 then,
and my girlfriend was home from school near Boston,
lying, probably, in her one-button jeans,
on that flowered, oversized couch
in her grandmother's cantilevered living room,
staring out at Lake George.
I knew the ice was still bare on the lake.
Maybe I had been dreaming we could
skate over between Long Island and Assembly Point,
go down past John's parents' house
where the summer guests had drained their pipes and left,
where no one would be watching,
before I turned and Freddie was there.
Who knows?

What I do remember was that catatonic silence
after we hit,
how I could stare up at the mute steel overhead
and hear nothing outside me.
I felt the ice radiating up
through my red and black jersey,
freezing its number 2 forever into my back —
second-born after Jim,
afraid I'd be second-dead after Tommy,
second without any doubt
in the eyes of my grandmother's God —
and so I scrambled to my feet.
Freddie Plunkett was knocked cold.
Two jagged stumps stuck up from his head
like broken, white pickets after a wild Halloween.

I couldn't tell what they were
until I touched my mouth.

In 1970,
Freddie's kidneys failed.
For a year they let him keep going,
shuffling blood
first into one scarred forearm and then the other,
red for black,
as he got ready to leave.
When he died,
I wrote a metaphorical elegy
about explorations and pioneers:
"Now your death has settled
like news of a new country in me," I said.
I couldn't see then what I needed to say.
That day, though,
none of us knew what would happen to anyone.
"You'll be all right," Coach Morrison said,
and he grinned to highlight his gaps.
"Join the man's club."
I wiggled my teeth out of Freddie's forehead,
and shoved them back into my gums.

Don't tell me my teeth didn't grow back.

Don't tell me they've stopped racing cars
over the deep ice
on Lake George in January.

Don't tell me Charlie Morrison
is a talkshow celebrity anywhere at all,
even in Albuquerque.

And don't tell me Freddie Plunkett
isn't skating around
some divine, glacial island
right now,
no down parka, no scarf —
just two ribbons of iridescent light
streaming wildly
from his glittering forehead.

2

It is the great past, not the dizzy present,
that is the best door to the future.

— Camille Paglia

IN THE NEW WORLD

Jabez Fitch, born Feb. 26, 1737 in Norwich, Ct., served during two years, 1756–1758, at Fort Edward, N.Y., in the French and Indian War. His diary from his second year there survives. His mother, Elizabeth Ballard Fitch, sailed to America from Devon, in England, with her husband, Daniel, in 1736. Her letter is to her own mother, who has asked to join Elizabeth in New England.

September—1757

Seven days now brisk cannon at Lake George
        & Col. Webb sends no one.
Colyer's prisoner claims 6000 Regulars, 5000 Canadians.
        Morning of the 10th, Major Prevos took
300 men & kept the lines the full day,
        meeting our people alive from the Fort.
Without firelocks & naked, most reached our bridge
        by noon; wounded were found
& carried in past sunset. We learned
        soon how they had been used:

first, were let surrender, assured of safety, when
        no encouragement came from us.
Were to take arms & packs with Colors Flying,
        & guarded as they left by French Regulars.
But as they marched out the Regulars fell back & Indians
        beset them, using spears.
Children they stole, opening their small heads on rocks,
        & their mothers afterwards & husbands
who would relieve them. The bodies left out then,
        cut & stripped like beef-cows.

19th. I work still with 20 men on the hospital.
          This day we found
Henry Shuntup, lost a week, on the wood-trail.
          His heart was torn out,
a large wood-knot lodged in its ragged chamber.

                                        14th March 1758
          My dear mother,

               You will fear I have entirely
               forgot you, when the opposite is more nearly
               the truth. I spy you 100 times each day,
               nodding off at church with Mrs. Frye,
               in the pie stalls at Willicombe,
               in and out of cleaned rooms.

               We are halfway into March here,
               and your letter from last September
               reached me only now. Daniel heard
               storms chased the Sea Flower
               all through her crossing, and likewise
               kept her off New London port, below us.

               Fall is the wrong time of year
               to sail for New England. Of 134
               who six months past left Liverpool,
               but 46 have landed alive and well.
               So with no reply from me, I fear
               you expect all are massacred here.

We are not. All of us but Daniel,
whose fingers stiffen, seem well
enough. He hides his pain from me,
or thinks he does, though I can see
how he lets a mallet slip
in mid-swing, how he often drops

a plane partway through a cut. He pounds
the work then with his clenched hands,
and I blame Mr. Huntington,
who cares less for the hands of his workmen
than he does for the foolish snow
on his cursed sloops. "Stay to houses, I know,"

Daniel throws back at me. "When no one builds
from October straight on through April,
where would we stand without Huntington
and his ships?" So there is little to be done.
Perhaps, after the war, if enough come back
there will be buildings again to make.

Jabez, two Junes ago, joined the war. He went
with a witless man, John Reynolds, a Captain
in the Volunteers. I acted the fool, crying
as he left, but I see all my children dying
night after dread night in my dreams,
or that is how it has come to seem

after Mary's death. And I remember
your crying when I chose to sail here.
I can see now, though, Daniel is right:
the French work hard to drive us out,
and someone's son must go. New Britain,
close by, has lost three women to their Indians.

October

15th. Considerable writing; a letter from mother
        dated the 4th. During Exercise,
we were startled by a smart firing from where Buckley's
        carpenters work, the guns sounding
near half an hour before Lyman sent a squad.
        Only one died, a New York man,
& not until nightfall. His name was Amos Rice,
        of Capt. Edwards company.
I remember him whipped on the 12th, 50 hard stripes,
        for sleeping at his post.

23rd. I have been this morning 16 months a Volunteer.
        Moses Cleavland said the Devil
removed bodily a soldier of the 17th, for a pact
        made two years past.
I took an account for a letter to Elisha.
        48 oxen swam the river.
About this time my dreams & thoughts
        work strange, of friends
& my family at home: I prepare for the worst
        with hymn & prayer.

Rain through three days now has saved
        the execution.
Afternoon, the *25th:* Colyer's prisoner was stepped
        through the Guards, a thousand
in two lines, facing. His uniform was left him,
        but with a white cap
& black ribbon. As he walked, he paled, gazing
        into a small book.
I observed him shut it more than once & fold
        his hands tight to his neck.

His coat stripped, he kneeled, watching
      the Grenadiers.
At first shots, he fell partly on one side
      of his head, the left,
but after some time made motions with one hand.
      Many re-loaded, yelling,
thinking he had survived & fired into him
      while he was quite dead.
He was a Dutchman named Peck, shot first
      from past ten yards.

Ebenezer Green has begun a weekly
named *The Norwich Summary,*
filled mostly with boiling sermons
and chilling news of war campaigns:
each week I follow down Green's list,
searching in the dead columns for Fitch,

then to J. for Jabez, and inside me my heart
leaps each time at not finding it,
as if some dark hand damming the course
of a tiny stream had been mercifully forced
away, and the water let flow once again.
I feel I can laugh, or at least breathe then.

So I buy some maple drops, or more
if I have annoyed a better customer.
This week I brought home a hymnbook,
Watt's Psalms, for you, and with luck
you may have it before summer is past.
I have two now, and one will last

me, as you know, my whole fallen lifetime.
I fear Daniel and I have missed our prime.
Jabez was twenty this last February.
He dwarfs Daniel now, and Mary
will be nine this month, if I add her four
cemetery years. Oh, mother,

I am full grown; what keeps me at forty
from letting her go? Forgive me.
I stay too much at home, and Daniel tells
me I mourn far too long. So I mind well
my plentiful, unending housework.
I would let no neighbor bark

that Elizabeth Fitch is a bad wife:
not one morning in our Norwich life
has he left the house in a ripped shirt,
nor, on his return, found the table short
of a full meal. And yet he complains
I nurse the baby still. How do I explain

to him a baby is not able, at two,
to give his mother up. "No, it is you,"
he shouts. "You want it. The boy would have quit
your breast last year." So, "Give him a brace and bit.
Give him a chisel if he's so well-grown,"
I answer back. Daniel has slept alone

since James was born, and holds his choice against me,
as if my crying kept him off his sleep.
I miss him, but I can no more
push James off early than wish Jabez killed in war.
Nature has left us women what is private
and enduring, mother. I rejoice in that.

November

11th. This first snow of Fall pulled the river-growth
         into the banks. Before sunset
I walked, staring up through the smoky air
         at the sun. North of it,
as I stood there, the sky became black rings
         of cannon smoke & inside
turned a fire of horses, as if heads & hooves
         had been stitched together & shot
from iron barrels. The bodies flashed apart
         & re-formed, into painted

cavalry, with their riders dead or fallen off.
         I judged it lasting 2 minutes,
before it grew unsteady & drew away.
         It seemed most like a dream
so strange I fear bad tidings from father.

December

14th. Trees in the wood keep falling from ice-weight.
         The crashing snaps through the fog
as if the sea were near & ships fell on rocks.
         Warm for the month,
it rained some. I hope for a letter from home.
         25th: Near 8 I heard
odd noises. A fire, as I ran out,
         had used the barracks
nearest the drawbridge. Only the frame stood,
         lining the night.

With water & snow we had the blaze
          most out by 12,
but feared many times for the magazine with the wind.
          A dog was caught in a cellar,
but no men were lost. I was planning
          what memorandum to mark
Christmas by, but now the fire will recall it.
          I think in such season a man
might observe his past & the overturns seen,
          & thus shape a judicious mind.

29th. I think last night the coldest I ever knew,
          with a strange light in the air
much like the one Nov. last. This opened
          in the East, then carried
round to the North, I was informed later.
          This morning I feel
obliged to observe my dreams, which ran
          vastly on flowered gardens,
as in May. I never heard these dreams fail,
          but what some horror followed.

          Elisha hardly ever visits home.
          He is apprenticed on a farm
          near Torrington, and betrothed to a girl
          named Lydia Trumbull. Two years he quarreled
          with us at every opportunity,
          so let him seek his own community

of friends. Let him marry and raise a child.
When he needs help he'll mark how worthwhile
his family was. I must tell you,
before I forget, James said he flew
across the sea, to your house, in my dream
last night. This morning I heard him scream

with delight. His face was perched above mine
as I awoke, and when I opened my eyes,
he flapped his arms and tried to crow.
He swooped down and plucked at my nose
with his mouth, or tried to, until he pitched
over. Then he wriggled under my quilt like a fish.

February—1758

8th. If a man step off the sleigh-track in wood-gathering,
        snow will take him to the waist.
Since 9 this day men worked at the far end
        of the new road, with nothing save
a covering party, 40 rods from the fort's gates.
        The Indians, wearing snowshoes,
seemed to drop from the oaks there, for none on watch
        saw them appear before
they heard their fire. They attacked where the sleigh
        sat within a small hollow.

In full sight of us, but past range of our muskets,
        our men were killed there,
or, caught without snowshoes, dragged calling out
        for us into the woods,

where the heathens tomahawked and scalped them,
    or carried them off
to gratify themselves later at their camp.
    I am 20 years on this,
my birthday, the 26th. Today, as well, eight months
    from home as a soldier.

Major Reynolds, once our neighbor, who made
    us laugh & sport so often,
was left at the first rim of woods this terrible dawn,
    his heart too a round stone
wedged in by the savages. Our enemy rejoices
    in serving us these miseries.
I have now a sharp fever & pains in my back & head,
    but dream of riding with Elisha
at home, coursing the green hills, though I can barely
    stand beside my hut door.

        Your last question wants an answer still.
        I can furnish you with how I feel,
        yet feelings pay no passage fares.
        Simply put, Daniel hands me no more
        than what will keep the household fit.
        Whether his income will admit

        our living in the manner we do,
        with one more added, I am stranger to.
        I know nothing of Daniel's money affairs.
        First, obtain a quote on your furniture,
        for you would need none to abide
        here, with us. And that may provide

the full amount for your crossing.
Besides some grandchildren, the only things
I can guarantee are snow
and my love. I need to say what you know
sometimes, if only to hear the word.
But what, after all, would Norwich offer?

We have two spacious commons
for grazing, four well-stocked inns,
each, they claim, serving Demerary rum,
and an Old Lights church you will feel at home
in. George Whitefield has twice preached
there. Last December, it was part beast,

part devil and part man he called the assembled.
Our Reverend Baldwin cried out he resembled
none of these, that he was pressed in God's mold,
and saw little need to be told
otherwise. At that, Mr. Whitefield reconsidered,
at least a moment, before he delivered

his final judgement: "I take this occasion
to correct my error. I was mistaken,"
he said. "You are not part anything.
You are entirely devil." And we have coveting,
for entertainment, as well. Whether
you could locate a new husband here,

it seems all is possible. Polly Baker,
of New Haven, when brought before
a court on her fifth flagrant charge
of bearing a bastard child, so moved the judge
she was pardoned, and married the next day
this same judge. "Does not the Bible say,"

she asked, "to increase and multiply?
Nothing can prevent me from that duty.
I should have, instead of a pillory,
a statue erected to my memory."
This truly is a new world, mother.
If you are able to raise your fare,

we will make do when you arrive.
But wait until we all survive
this war, and let Daniel raise a list
of trustworthy captains and ships.
The risk of an untried vessel is too great.
I think it foolish not to wait

until summer. I must leave off now,
and make a hasty pudding for tomorrow.
It is past midnight. I think of you always.
Pray, and try not to be frightened for us.
We shall be happy if circumstance allows it.
We shall pass our time together yet.

> Your loving daughter,
> Elizabeth

March

11th. Lt. Pratt arrived here this night
      from Saratoga, with news
of smallpox there, but no letter for me.
      6 days of rain,
& strange flies hatch from the floorboards.
      Isaac Andrus stood my guard.

Near midnight I heard the pickets shoot at wolves.
  Now I mark how the ice
shivers & moans, breaking up in the river.
  I am too sick to walk.

13th. 30 wagons from Albany, with scaling ladders,
  have come. I return with them,
& then on to Conn., to find my health again.
  Sunday, the *15th*, Canaan:
Dr. Billings gave me a stern potion of ipecac
  & afterwards carried me
out into his meadow to follow the sunset.
  An unaccountable noise
inhabited the air, matching the report of 2 cannons.
  An abundance of pigeons fled.

Mrs. Donica mixed herbs & applied them
  through the incessant night.
An old, single-legged man tarried by me also,
  telling of the Iroquois.
They stole him when a child & made him theirs
  through what he named
a sweat-lodge. I slept much, hearing only parts,
  though once I woke
to find him singing over me. I am sure I forget most.
  A dream, though, answering him,

so remarkable I must make some note of it.
  I had dragged flat stones,
one by one, up from a dry, distant riverbed,
  past a tent of curved poles.
I balanced them over a fire, feeding in strips
  of my own peeled skin.

When the stones glowed, I poured water onto them,
      & the steam thickened,
building a ribbed hut around me. I lay inside a horse then,
      tearing at his long bones until I woke.

❧

THE SLAVE SHIP

J.M.W. Turner based his painting on an account of what occurred on the slave ship Zong *in 1781. Luke Collingwood was captain, and he sailed with a crew of 14 and a cargo of 400 slaves.*

During their passage from Africa to Barbados, an epidemic raged on board and, before they encountered a storm near Jamaica, they had almost run out of fresh water. Collingwood later told a court that the slaves had brought the disease onto his ship, and that his men needed the water to care for the cargo. His first mate, Kelsall, testified during the trial that Collingwood had said if the human cargo died of illness or thirst, they were not covered by insurance, but a jettison of the slaves was legal, and would be covered. Subsequently, 135 slaves were thrown into the ocean.

The London court's decision went against the insurance company, and the owners of the Zong *were paid "30 pounds per capita for the goods thrown overboard."*

The painting's first title was Slavers throwing overboard the dead and dying — Typhoon coming on. *The letter is based on reports made by Lt. John Matthews, who worked in Africa during the years 1785, 1786, and 1787.*

My dear friend,
I hope I am able, with this,
my last response, to finally lighten
your childish heart with a short analysis
of slaving, and to prove its necessity
for this hopeless continent of Africa.
What minor part of the Trade's history
is known by me would please you far less
than what I have seen, myself, along the river
called Sierra-Leone, and in this oppressive wilderness
that covers the coast. In my third year
of tropical life, what I have learned
of slavery shows our methods much less severe
than the natives' own, and, in the end,
leaves them more fortunate than most comprehend.

These upraised hands
and this one leg
upside down in the right foreground
the one exposed
mid-thigh to toe
as it slides down surrounded
by white fish
with bulging black eyes
and perfect hunger in their eager
upturned tails
these few extremities
easily mistaken for fish or waves
and caught
for this one instant
between the onrushing diagonal rain
and the torrential sea
that accepts
everyone
even this ship on the left
with its blood-red empty masts
tipping back
these evanescent strokes
are people
already almost completely under
the burnt umber and white-lead foam
flecked with hovering gulls
These bodies
you cannot see
were chained sideways
ass to face
alive or dead this morning
in the slippery hold you also won't see here
The blood
squeezed from their bodies

                    steamed up through
                           gratings
                  and became this swollen sky
                      that sweeps up here
                          to the left
                        upper corner
            Before the first ominous red of morning
                         a small boy
                   who dreamed of the moon
                    over his empty village
                          woke up
                           crying
                  Kickeraboo   Kickeraboo
                       We are dying
                       We are dying

From what history I have collected, each war
provides the victorious tribe,
if they be cannibals, with much more
than can be preserved, or, if planting-time,
with field-slaves. Most, if taken after harvest,
die. For almost any crime,
natives will sell a man, if they let him live.
If not made household or harem slaves,
before we Europeans came, these captured natives
could only hope to remain strong
each year when planting-time returned.
Believe me, slaves have been used here as long
as people have walked. Now, at least, as our boats
sail, the natives sell before they cut slaves' throats.

Most mornings
they were danced on deck
in ankle chains
like this one in the right foreground
still attached
to flesh
and these other disembodied
iron loops
that float here
for no reason
in the
quiet center
like magenta question marks
forged shut
below these hands
still raised
above the knife-smoothed waves
As the Captain slept
the sailors
even sober might laugh
Some would
wash down the women they wanted
and take them
there
the ones the Captain
no longer wanted
Some would order the men in irons up
Jump
some would shout
or
move your feet
though those with swollen ankles
might bleed to death

from dancing
and the sailor with the cat-o'-nine-tails
be flogged then
A toothless woman might bang
an upturned kettle
and the fool who signed on at Liverpool
to play bagpipes
on the Guinea slaver
for a quarter-percent share
might try a reel
to make the crew forget what they all do
as the dancers
sing their own words for
sorrow
for child
The smell
whatever shit or vomit
or rubbed-raw blood
might still cling
to the chained men
or half-grown boys
would be flushed past the coiled ropes
and the sea would sing
on quieter mornings
to the dancers
silently
across these purple waves
Come home
I am the way home
Come home

Apart from crimes and war, slaves are caught
and sold in numerous ways. Most European coastal
dealers who buy inland have brought
rum to dash the maniacal witch
doctors, who then rush through the village,
pointing out by their smell the ones in which
the black magic resides. Many
tribal kings claim all the village maidens
as wives, then pay spies to name any
who act adulterous. In corn-fields, children
scaring birds are often kidnapped. Fathers
even sell their families in times of famine
to see them fed. Now, though, these kings grow greedy:
I have seen some who sell their own children into captivity.

But this morning
the air-holes and wind-sails
were fastened tight
stiff tarpaulins
yanked
over the coated gratings
to keep this ghostly spray
that buoys the ship here
from filling the hold
and the surgeon
was sent down
amidships
to force-feed the tallest men first
Two cutlass-armed sailors
rammed
moldy plantains
awash in palm oil

or mashed yams filled with maggots
into whatever could still move
but resisted
eating
So many fainted from heat
or noxious vapors
and so much blood and mucous
coated the floor
none could reach the waste buckets
and the surgeon
remembered
a slaughterhouse
he had worked in as a boy
Just before
the surgeon himself fainted
by the ladder
and had to be dragged up
the slave closest
bit into his foot and held on so hard
a toe came away
The slaver crossed this angry line
of light and foam
the absent sun had called to its horizon
The typhoon swirled closer
and the dead
pitched
in the hold
some still nestled
manacled spoon-like
two by two with the living
none of us can see
here

From inland the slave coffles wind along
the river-ways to the coast,
each slave slung to another with a leather thong
frogged at the neck, thirty or more in a string,
with an elephant's long tusk or a packet of corn
balanced on every head. The traders bring
them then to middle factors, or some days sell directly
to the slaver captains. These raucous sales
I have enjoyed myself, many times, watching each party
take great pains to avoid worthless goods.
The dealers' men shave and sleek the tired slaves
with palm oil to hide old age, or they stuff wads
of oakum in them to halt their bloody flux,
while the ships' surgeons scurry to root out tooth decay or pox.

On this morning
Collingwood is awake
sitting at his carved table
easing pork chops down with English brandy
Two slaves
a woman
he remembers giving beads to afterwards
and a strong Fulani
with a nose broken the first day out
for trying suicide
both weak
from dysentery or scurvy
bound to chairs
are being fed from the Captain's table
Note this
he is saying to Kelsall

as a sailor
drains a tankard of rum into the man's mouth
held open
with a pair of hot tongs
Jamaican rum
Collingwood goes on
what we reserve for dashing Susu kings
Nothing
is too good
for our guests on the Zong
Note well
Mr. Kelsall
I would sooner we all die of thirst
than lose
the smallest
member of our cargo

When sales are through, buyers mark the ones
they own, scalding each owner's unique mark
into chests or backs with an incandescent iron.
Then they beat them toward the beach
with hide whips and most, glimpsing an ocean
for the first time, will beseech
the slavers to kill them there, or will clutch
howling at the sand until the native Krumen
drag them to the transport boats. Inasmuch
as the slaves think whites are new kings, who would sell
them to cannibals, they will jump
to waiting sharks or, with their chains, try to strangle
themselves. Some captains report that Ibos
have hanged themselves at their first sight of Barbados.

Somewhere
in these accents of light
against mist and vapor and symbolic blood
the sun
some luscious knot
of broken vermilion
is slashing an angry path
Or maybe
since we are not shown it here
the sun
a round daub
of variegated red lead
somewhat bigger than a shilling
waits
And again
since we should not forget
painting is a continuous inquiry
into relationships
between form
light
color
and the immaterial vehicles
of half-dissolving steam
ultramarine smoke tempered with copal
and half-veiled mist
all of which can suggest
of course
fragments of sky ship sea or human body
somewhere in here then
perhaps

in a huddled line
starting at the stern rail
and coiling along the foam-battered
starboard side
are what remain of
135 pairs
of open eyes
we have simply not found yet
These eyes that try not to notice
the swirling vortical curves
waiting below
or the indistinct air
heavy with the approaching storm
these eyes that try not to hear
the half-finished
screams
swallowed up in frenzied splashing
these eyes press their hands into
their neighbors' hands
and they sing

Thank you for these essays. I have so little here
to read, yet, oddly, all I need to stay drunk.
I daresay you favor the brand of writer
who harps on the grave inhumanity
of our Slave Trade, while summering near Dover.
If they hold mankind is equal, let them come visit me.
The whole of this immense continent
is as a wilderness stocked with black wolves.
They would see. We fear God. We are different
than slaves and beasts, who are links in Nature's

chain, at best. You will think what you must.
I am of the mind that Providence prefers
we save these creatures from certain death in their country,
and change them into useful members of our society.

What you can see here
is the dream
beginning
the dream of the living
left on board
the ship
Their screams arch up and out
of them as they fall
mixing brown
and red
catching among these turbulent swells
so easily
you would swear they were only
what wind
can sound like
caged in relentless water
or punished water
angering itself
against terrified wind
You can see
these upraised hands
straining still
in the vaporous air and ochre light
leaving one final sign
Look
there is nothing hidden now

Look
they are waving
calling
to the ones
left listening on deck
or floating in the dark hold
They are waving
to the gathering mist of jib
and skewed masts
reeling off sideways
They are waving
to Collingwood and Kelsall
Go ahead
these hands say
cross into the white foam of your future
Go ahead
you will be left with
yourselves
and the full memory of our eyes
burning
in all of our
childrens'
eyes
They are waving
to us
They are waving
as they start home
and the cries
of the diving
white gulls
are disappearing
overhead

THE ISLAND OF BIRDS

Captain Jacques Cartier made three voyages of discovery to North America — in 1534, 1535, and 1541. In all of these, he sailed from the port of St. Malo on the coast of Brittany, encouraged by King Francis I to find not only new territories for France, but also to bring back from the New World what the Spaniards had been finding there: gold and precious gems, as well as other commodities valued by the Europeans.

On the second voyage, during the exploration of the St. Lawrence River, all of Cartier's three ships became stuck in the ice near what became St. Croix, and they were unable to move for six months. There were no European settlements to which they could march, so they built a fort around their ships and wintered where they were. Almost all of Cartier's men got scurvy, and many died there.

Donnaconna, chief of the friendly Hurons, beguiled Cartier with tales of a kingdom called Saguenay, inhabited by white men who could fly like bats, ingested only liquids, and tended vast gold mines. Cartier, believing him, persuaded the Huron chief to accompany him back to France, where Donnaconna convinced King Francis I as well. This insured the monarch's financial backing for a third voyage, but France's on-going war with Spain, and the stories of the winter hardships during the second voyage, made adventurous sailors hard to find.

Marc Jalobert, one of the captains on this second voyage, was Cartier's brother-in-law. Neither of them was related to the sailor who speaks here.

Go ahead, John. Sail with him, as you please.
        But keep a weather eye
on Cartier and his brother-in-law. You'll share
no Saguenay diamonds or gold. Marc Jalobert
        could go and pry
the King's fat thighs apart, squeeze

        his plums till the royal tongue waxed blue,
                and still Cartier
        could save his pompous, privileged head.
        Marc winnowed out a useful bride to wed.
                For all of us, let's say,
        common seamen, and that brig swallows you,

and me, our skins, with an eighth-point share
                of salted auks
or giant tortoise shells, are the most we'll take
home. Or maybe you'll rage all night, awake,
                when you come back
like me. I still can feel the leg I left there.

            Tell me. How do I remember pain from that?
            Anoudasco
        is the savages' word for leg. One of them
        found it, dragged it off to catch wampum.
                    That's all they know
        to want — their strung wampum beads. They cut a slit

in an enemy's chest, and buttock, and stomach, and thigh,
                then weight the body
with stones, and cast it to the bottom
of the river, where they know the wampum,
                in half a day,
will occupy each bloody gash. Aye,

            you're right to gasp. I once saw a healthy
                    man killed and lowered
        just so, and I watched them haul him up again.
        He had become, God help me, a clanking chain
                    of those creatures.
        I'll wager my leg made some Huron boy wealthy.

From mid-October through last March we stuck,
                all three ships, in amid
river-ice. *Honnesca*, they call it. You can know no world
so quiet as that. Water in all the casks on board,
                overnight, grew solid.
Ice at the gunwales was a hand-breadth thick.

As far in a day as one of us could walk,
                    the river lay set. Before
Christmas, we learned a pestilence had come
in among the savages. By their word, some
                    fifty of their number
had died, and at that, we charged they take

themselves from our ships and fort, and come near
                    us no more. Still it cast
among us, though, like some spirit that needs no touch
to spread itself, and with stark afflictions such
                    as none had seen — some lost
all strength, and on some others there would appear

                    spots of blood, that seeped if opened, but purple. Many
                            could not stand. Their limbs
                    would swell and freeze, and their sinews shrink, black
                    like burned rope. Up ankles and legs to the neck
                            blood-spots increased. Their gums
                    rotted; teeth broke off; tongues swelled. Any

who could walk would not so quickly swell and freeze.
                    By January, the sickness
had multiplied, so that not more than seven men
were left sound in all our three ships. Our Captain
                    ordered, in the wilderness,
a man-sized image raised, between the fir trees,

                    of Christ, less than a gun-shot from our fort-gates.
                            He commanded us,
                    whole or sick, to pray there on that Sunday,
                    the eighteenth, that the Lord might evidence some way
                            to ease our perilous
                    state, and named himself, if we witnessed it abate,

a devout pilgrim to the Holy Virgin upon
                    his return to France.
No sooner was service done than our boyhood friend,
Philip Rougemont, spun about, as if he should defend
                    himself. He advanced
upon Jalobert, cursing him, calling out words none

          of us could comprehend, and then, as suddenly,
                    fell to his knees,
          held forth his hands, and died. So Cartier had us rip
          him open, nape to gullet, and bade us strip
                    what skin the disease
          had colored black — all this to show what malady

gripped us so tight, and uncover the nature
                    of our plague. We found
his heart spoiled, and white, with near a quart
of red circling round it, as in that still port
                    the ice fenced us round.
His lungs lay mortified, but his liver fair.

          What we saw of his spleen was most perished,
                    rough as if ground
          between stones, and his skin, though black without,
          seemed unspoiled beneath. Listen, I tell you about
                    him, thus, only to pound
          into your foolish head what might happen there. I wished

then that God had called me instead, and many times
                    after Philip as well —
each time we tore a man open, or packed
one under snow, waiting there for the ice to crack
                    and the snow to melt,
each of us hoping, by turns, for death or Springtime.

By early March, but two could climb below,
                    to melt water
or care for the sick. They were William Britton
and Cartier. We left our dead out, or piled one
                    upon another
by then, under sails, when our strength would allow.

Amid all this, our Captain grew afraid
                    the inhabitants,
friendly as they seemed, would see our misery
and plan to attack us. To try and guarantee
                    each day our settlement's
safety, the two of them would sometimes parade

          outside the gates, or Cartier might hurl stones
                    at Britton, who dressed
          in varied clothes, and shout, to show the savage people
          our men must labor caulking the ships still,
                    and could not rest
          until they had finished. To sharpen the tone

of this play, he would order all the men
                    inside, whole or sick —
aloudeche, all the sick men — to furnish sounds
with hammers, or hands, or whatever sticks we found.
          Oh, John, at this sad trick,
I lost all hope of seeing my France again.

          My life, which I had to that sorry point held
                    so rich, with harbors
          full of new alehouses, and the safe emptiness
          of a dark sea at night, and the ready flesh
                    of a thousand whores
          I had sought out, soured. All my memories swelled

into an agony of constant dreams. Once I saw
                    my mother standing
over me, holding out a baby I knew
was me — a baby, *exiasta*. A crow flew
                    out of his crying
mouth, then landed and began to draw

          forth veins from my swollen leg, the lost leg I shout
                         for now. And there
          were others. The dead near me rose up, black,
          then turned to a white fire flowing like candle-wax
                    all together,
          and from that white fire long fingers reached out

toward those who might still be living.
                    Adanahoe,
my mother. *Athau*, cold. *Amocdaza*,
a dead man. Under the earth, *conda*.
          We shall all go
toward the stars, *Stagnehoham*. In my dying,

          I fashioned what life I never had —
                    a decent woman
          appeared, with strong children who ran
          across a sunlit field, and I was able to stand
                    and watch them, or run
          alongside. And I imagined a useful trade,

pottery, where I could stay close to fire.
                    I built a whole house
in my mind, one that faced out upon the ocean.
Then one day, in search of food, the Captain
                    met along the ice
Donnaconna, the chief who just ten days before

he had seen near death from our same sickness.
          To mask the spread
of the disease among us, he claimed his serving-man
was so afflicted, and asked what cured such poison.
          Donnaconna led
him then to a tree, snapped off three branches,

and directed him thus — to boil the leaves and bark,
          serve the cooled liquid,
and wrap with the dregs the swollen body.
Afraid at first for the bitter taste, we
          passed the cure amid
us, joking that, with our skins gone dark,

          we were Saguenay bats already. Soon, though, when all
                    could stand and walk,
          and when some, pox-marked from other countries
          four years or more, grew free of their disease,
                    a tree as thick
          as any oak was axed, lopped bare, and boiled.

All of us were healed so, and the river,
          with perilous shrieks,
gave up her ice but one week later. At the end
of March, we set off, and reached Newfoundland
          within two weeks,
carrying with us Donnaconna and his brother.

          Fourteen leagues off that mainland, we came
                    to a small island,
          which we called the Island of Birds, for this
          reason — though you hear me say it, John, unless
                    you could go stand
          among their numbers, you would surely claim

me a liar. While only a league around,
                    the island is covered
by birds, a hundred fold, with as many hovering
about it as within. Because their wings
                    are no bigger
than half your hand, they fly close to the ground.

          They are the size of jays, but black and white,
                    with beaks like crows,
          and are fat as pigeons. Weak as we still were,
          we waded in among them to provision our return.
                    The lightest of blows
          to the head would kill them, and so few took flight

that in one hour two boats were loaded full.
                    I had strapped a beech limb
along my thigh to help me walk, but its end,
time and again, caught in the wet sand.
                    So I clung to a boat-rim,
weak and sickened, and heard the dreadful

          flaps and cries. And I saw, John, I swear,
                    the faces of our dead
          upon those birds. I fell then, crawled, and began
          to swim toward the ship. I heard laughter, and the Captain
                    shouting for me. Someone said,
          "Let him drown." Then someone else: "Fetch him back here."

                              ⌇

3

Sometimes I think I got that Christ look. I think I was God in school. I went to the convent, but they didn't teach me much. I'm gonna be Christ until judgment day. That'll be in 2000. Maybe things will change then. I think we'll see a sign.

— Mabel, aka the Sea Hag, at the YWCA

STORIES. REAL ONES.

1

I had a friend named Raymond Alberelli.
Sounds like the boss of a crime family, eh?
He was an 8 year old
on Fulton St. my father killed.
Suddenly, between parked cars, Ray ran straight out,
like some bag kicked up by wind, my dad thought.
It was the first week in June, a Saturday.
Jesus. Who that you know knows when they'll die?
Ray missed a thrown ball maybe,
laughed, I'll bet, and acted silly
before he turned and took off after it.
My old man had no idea what he'd hit.

He works now at staying awake,
all the time, and he walks. He tries to walk
the night away, to avoid me, or my mother.
He claims he was daydreaming about her
when he heard the thump. He started to stop,
saw a pigeon swerve unsteady and then lift up,
and figured that was probably all.
Until he looked in his mirror and saw Ray roll
off to the side. I was in Wynantskill,
last week, at Mike's house, and saw my father walk by. "Mil,"
my mom's name, he was saying to himself, "those sheets —
there's blood. You see the blood I left on those new sheets?"

2

Dear Mrs. Cameron,

Thank you ever so much
    for the sterling silver relish and pickle dish.
      Its overlaid leaves and vines are so lush.
    It's truly quite beautiful.
        How can I thank you enough?

Angelo really adores
    red pepper relish, Polish dills and kosher spears —
      though I buy less now he's sworn off hamburgers.
    Past age thirty-five, he groans,
        food gets so much harder.

It's butter chips I crave.
    Just between us, they're best after making love.
      And your dish has perfect depth. The moment it arrived,
    we could both tell that it would be,
        well, special. What a prize!

Do you like pickles? Relish?
    Probably. Next time, after you and Mr. Cameron finish,
      why not give it a whirl. But not in a rush —
    slowly, and, most important, together.
        Otherwise it's over in a flash.

Oops, isn't that just like me,
    hopping to conclusions, presuming you're exactly
      like us. Maybe you and Mr. Cameron don't, anymore. Maybe
    pickles aren't really at the top
        of your list. I think they should be.

No, wait, that sounds absurd.
　　I'm not writing to say that at all. Rest assured
　　　　we love it, we do, naked or not. It will be treasured.
　　　　　What more could a couple of newlyweds ask?
　　　　In pickle dishes, it's the last word.

3

It was just a hot afternoon with no clouds up at 8000.
She jumped last and the pilot thought later
some updraft maybe,
some bump that could spill your apple juice on a DC–10,
probably caught her off-guard
and hammered her head into the jump-door rim.

Her husband Jim had wanted to jump first.
Swears he was too far under to help.
He swears he heard her head smack
that rim, swears he looked back and saw her burst
free of the sideways plane then.
So she twirled toward him in a wild, forced

homecoming, her blood caterwauling like a lost compass
toward the magnetic, braced earth.
Some of them tried to catch air and slow.
Terry came closest.
She climbed so near she heard the sleeves flapping,
then had to feel herself miss.

In the time it would take to wash our hands, or to follow
Mom's grace, or to see the heart of some wrong-headed bird
in her palm had stopped clamoring,
or even to chew a mouthful of peanuts, and swallow,
my sister,
for that same ordinary time, fell.

4

one time japanese beetles
ate off every bite of my skin
but i didn't die
i was still moving in my body
look right here
this is where the first one bit me
actually japanese beetles
can ruin your long pants
they can pinch away with their pinchers
all of where your knee goes
like mine right here where they ate it
i'm not kidding
i found a baby squirrel by our porch
in norfolk virginia
i named him wiggles
a storm with no thunder
knocked him out of his treetop
we found his three brothers too
curled up in the black branches that flew down
but not opening their feet
he lived in my sneaker box
and i put small drops of milk in his mouth
but mom said only when he moved his legs and squeaked
so he wouldn't explode
i don't know if he liked me or not
his eyes never got open
i helped my dad make a song for him

rock a bye wiggles
squirrels can't fly
drink all your milk
or you're gonna die
and i sang it a lot too every day
so it wasn't my fault
i dug a grave near the swamp where i can't walk
with my yellow beach shovel
and i gave wiggles a beetle for his trip
my dad has my three uncles
uncle steve who lives with us
and another one
jim who forgot our names
and uncle david
who has a big head like wiggles
my dad took uncle david to a special school once
back in the dark ages he said
when he was a kid
and he got really scared
of somebody in a wheelchair
with a football helmet
who couldn't keep his arms straight
to put food in his mouth
and he grabbed my dad's arm and held on
maybe my dad was scared
he was hungry and would take bites of his arm
uncle david has too much water stuck inside his head
dad said
i'm not scared of anything
i'm not kidding
look at this green bug
do you see him

he's in the folded over part
he's not a green bug
he's a cricket
look he's putting his hands on the flower
don't touch that
i grabbed a thorn once
and it dug a hole in my finger
you have to keep looking and looking every minute
for anything sharp pointing up
i want a japanese beetle for uncle david
can you help me catch one
let's see if one's in here
nope not here
nothing
look this flower's opened out too wide
smell it
right here is where nectar lives

5

There are worse things than cancer.
Like deep-sea fishing with my ex-husband for a week.

After Missouri —
you laugh, Joan, but it's true —
after my bone-marrow transplant,
I came back here and I was on cloud nine.
Mandy was engaged. The kids were healthy. I was alive.

Then Jack came over.
He was trying to be decent.
He had brought chateaubriand for a barbecue
and he spent an hour getting the charcoal perfect.
He gave Mike a long ride in his new demonstrator Lexus.

Sitting there,
watching him cook the steak,
I started to feel sucked down again,
like I was re-entering that relentless whirlpool
of new cars, cocktail parties, bonus-point Bimini vacations.

He couldn't even hug me.
I know he has a different family now,
but we had twenty years and four kids together.
And then I got angry with myself for wanting him back.
I was way past being a car dealer's perky, Junior League wife.

Anyway, I'm bald.
Cytoxan took care of that.
I don't have the right wife-look anymore.
Dr. Hawkes, my first oncologist, said, "Cytoxan's tough.
The ladies don't like Cytoxan because they lose all their hair."

"I'm not the *ladies*,"
I tossed back, "and I intend to live."
We get the disease, but they're all in charge.
"Oh, let's see these tests, my my my, oh, here, sorry,
the only way to be sure is to take the entire breast right away.

"Sorry, better take both.
Sorry, Mrs. X, there's metastasis.
See this little spot here on the hip scan?
Chemotherapy is the only proven route I can offer.
Transplants are experimental; that means insurance won't pay."

What am I saying?
You don't want to hear this.
This is Mandy's wedding day, for God's sake.
I should be talking about grandchildren, right?
But I don't want to plan beyond this moment — here, today.

As far as I know,
I'm clean now. I'm okay.
But cancer is an insidious force.
It's like nothing you've experienced before.
When it starts out, you're afraid you'll lose body parts.

That's a joke.
Everything becomes relative.
By the second visit, you pray you'll just *live*.
There is a physical process you have to go through,
but you can become somebody new. You re-define yourself.

I am my mind,
and the spirit inside of me,
not just blood and bones and bad cells
that one fine day decided they'd break off from the rest
and began to stalk me, growing inside me, poisoning everything.

Relax, Joan.
You're turning green.
Do you really think I want to die?
When I was in Missouri, in the worst of it,
throwing up, spaced out on morphine, my mom was there.

Every two hours,
she woke me up to urinate.
Can't let heavy metals settle in your organs.
She monitored my saline drip, pressed my chemo pump,
picked up hair clumps so I wouldn't see them and completely freak.

She said to me,
in a moment I looked gone,
"Your mother won't leave you, you know."
I looked up from puking, smiled, and said back,
"Don't worry. I'll put in a good word if I wake up in heaven."

The hardest part
of dying is dealing with the kids.
I wrote them all letters before the transplant,
telling them about their births, how I named each one.
I had to find out, and let them know, what they really meant to me.

That seemed so final.
I had to give up on lying
to write my kids those last letters.
I had to believe I could really die, and accept it.
As soon as I did that, I felt myself actually come alive

for the first time.
I really see my kids now.
They're the best thing in my life.
I don't use my trouble as an excuse.
I look at them now and they're enough for me.

Cancer changed me.
It got me to finally wake up.
But it isn't a catalyst for everybody.
People think it makes your whole family act nice
all the time. Get a life. Michael's been angry for two days

over Tom's bachelor party.
He's fifteen. They had a stripper
and an open bar, and I wouldn't let him go.
He said, "You're dying. Does that mean *I* have to?"
It's hard to always remember someone else's disease.

I do have strange dreams.
I'll be standing in a familiar house
and a wall will blow out, with no warning,
or I might be dressing one of my kids for school,
and they'll melt into blood right there in my hands.

But some things are easy.
Cancer sets up a strange sisterhood.
It's like that old bumper sticker that said,
"Wouldn't it be great if schools had what they needed
and the Air Force had to hold bake sales to buy their planes?"

That isn't right,
but it was something like that.
We hold bake sales to save our own lives.
I don't mean to sound negative. I'm really not.
I have an odd sense of my life going on, no matter what,

even after my death.
It wouldn't matter to me
if today were my last day alive.
I think I believe that. What I do know is
I love my kids, and I'm a good mother. And I know

I'm tired of cancer.
I'm sick of waiting rooms.
It's like facing a weekly firing squad,
over and over. Tumor markers up again—
from 334 . . . to 567 . . . to 720 . . . and then where?

I bought three wigs.
My smile isn't phony now.
I don't have to be Miss America anymore.
I don't care about dirt and I don't cook every night.
I fill my teapot. I drink my tea. I'm happy if it stays down.

My cancer will spread until I stop it, or die. That's it.
Let's have some cake. Life's uncertain. Eat your dessert first.

6

I'm gonna share something with you.
I'm a recovering alcoholic.
And drugs, too.
I seen a lot, don't kid yourself.
One friend stone-fucking dead with a spike in
and still jumping, no shit,
twitching from the nerves working overtime, you know?

Don't try and tell me we ain't in no recession.
What's true is true and I am living goddamn proof.
I was in the printers' union,
that's why I come here five years back,
no other frigging reason but that.
Seniority, everyplace, that's your ticket to the races.
Five years ain't enough, not with local guys at ten.

Some of them got fifteen even.
Company got bought out, who you think went first?
So that's how come I'm stuck in this cab.
I'm gonna write down what I know from what I seen.
My ex tells me I got all this stuff locked inside of me, deep,
and not the washed-out crap you watch on TV.
Stories. Real ones. Family stories.

Like my old man pissing blood
straight onto our kitchen linoleum once.
Woke me out of a dead sleep.
I walk in and he's propped against the fridge,
holding his pecker and winking at me,
a fucking Bud crushed in his free hand.
"You want something to stare at?" he says.

Then he lets his head loll back and he hawks one on the ceiling,
and it stayed up there.
His pants were all the way down, covered up his shoes,
and he was laughing his bare ass off,
his ass muscles pumping in and out like he was breathing with it,
laughing like he wasn't afraid of God
or nothing else in this world.

❦

7

I remember
  it rained straight
    for a week
      and our crowned road
        that wound up
          from our picturesque trout stream
          collapsed
            that narrow summer
              just before she bailed out
                A log
                  rammed our bridge
                that time
                  and split a beam

                  The last morning
                    I thought
                      mourning doves were waking me
                    It was her
                      crying
                        She had squeezed
                          three drops of Krazy Glue
                      on her ass
                      and then backed
                      over against me
                    as I slept
                    Three drops
                  she said
                    one for each
                    unforgettable
                    year

8

Mister-hey-don't-bother-asking-
let-me-tell-you-I-know-everything-
but-oh-I'm-sorry-I'm-short-on-money-just-now?
He's married again, to some . . . Forget it. I know how
charming that slime could be. I don't blame you anymore,
but for my maid of honor, the night before
my wedding . . . I do wish you'd told me
sooner, though, and spared me those five, glorious, country
winters in distorted gene-pool land.
Head back to nature and make your stand
against, what was it we hated, conformity?
For us it was: Stake your claim on poverty.

Listen, I promised I'd never tell
this to anyone, but what the hell,
anything I can do to help him suffer.
We moved up there in early June, the summer
of '75, and camped out in a screen tent
while Paul Bonehead built his woodshop. Then we spent
the winter in that dump, with a woodstove and outhouse — hauling
water up from the creek. Yes, I heard condos calling
to me even back then. So Mister-Smart-and-Free
situates our outhouse off in the birch trees,
which worked, sort of, until snow arrived. Then you could
take your pick — hold it all night, or freeze your ass in the woods.

Well, this one night, mid-February, 35 below,
I felt him shifting. I knew he had to go,
but so what? Moving there was his idea.
I'm supposed to feel bad? Let him be a
mountain man, with his clean, mountain air. He rolled out,
finally, and I just snuggled deeper in. I was dreaming about

mice who published their own investing magazine,
but like some Ziegfeld follies chorus-line scene,
I still remember. Then I heard
his shovel scraping for a while, but that blurred
into the clank of the letterset press
the mice were running. You know, unless
I'm sorely mistaken, since a woman's frigidity
is grounds for divorce, blatant stupidity
should be considered by the courts, because
in the morning, when I opened the outhouse door, there he was,
hunched in his parka and frozen to the seat.

I guess he fell asleep and his body heat
melted the ice. But then I guess it re-froze.
"I can't get up," he said, "I think my toes
are frostbitten." I don't know what he expected
me to do, but what I selected
from my short list, which was laughing until I cried,
really pissed him off. He did have his pride
to consider. So next thing I knew, this audible rip
comes from inside, and a terrible groan. I bit my lip
to keep from exploding. And he stepped out,
calmly, and tried to walk away without
showing any pain. No matter what happened,
he'd be damned if he let you know it. Then I opened
the door and, I swear, this pink ring of skin
was lit up when I let the sunlight in.
I laughed so hard I fell backward, into the fresh snow,
and then I heard, in the quiet dawn, my laugh, and then its echo.

9

Listen, you say you're a salesman,
what does that mean?
You think you sell me this car that makes you one?
I'll kiss my own ass if that makes you one.
How old are you — 30, 32?
Okay, so you're 38. Now hold it, right there, that's you,
that's the exact thing I want to explain.
Attitude. Don't show me one second of your pain,

no embarrassment, no desire, no anger, nothing.
You want to sell me something, anything —
life insurance, a lame thoroughbred, a half-done condo
in a Florida swamp, there's only one thing you *can't* do —
let me know you need it.
The sale, I mean. You think that's bullshit?
Hey, you'll learn, you'll pay taxes, you'll die.
I never said you shouldn't talk about your life. Just lie.

The minute you admit anything real
about yourself — that's it. You start to feel
what happened, and then you're washed up. You lose control.
A good salesman never digs a hole
for himself. Learn psychology, or they'll bury you.
Learn what your customers like you to do,
then do it. Rapport is the only key
to a sure sale. Let me tell you a story.

This really happened, to Jerry Evans, almost ten years
ago now. You know him? He grew up here.
He ran this giant sporting goods store

up in Utica when I was Chevy dealer there.
We weren't what you'd call friends,
but he'd bought two cars from me, so, when
my kids wanted skis, or boots, or camping stuff,
I'd reciprocate. Not that it mattered. He had enough

to buy and sell me three times over.
Well, Jerry spent part of every winter
scuba diving with his boy. They'd photograph
sharks or shipwrecks, I guess, maybe coral reefs.
And they'd done it for years; they were pros.
Anyway, this last trip, the boy goes
inside a cave after an eel up ahead,
and he disappears. That was normal, Jerry said.

Hell, the boy had damn near grown up underwater.
He wasn't upset. But a few minutes later,
Jerry found the boy's watch.
Then he got frantic, and he started to search.
He looked until his air ran out. Back on shore,
the lifeguards launched their boat, and Jerry tore
up and down the beach, calling, tracking
every breaking wave, and finally asking

everyone he came across if they'd seen
any divers climb back out of the ocean.
He waited there where they'd first gone in,
hunched over, a towel wrapped around him,
hoping like some damn fool the whole night
that he was simply wrong, that everything was all right.
He'd magically forgotten. The boy hadn't come along
this trip. Just let his memory be wrong,

please, this one time, and he'd never ask again.
He said he must have dozed off then.
Something woke him, the sun, a gull, who knows.
He squinted and saw two porpoises
a hundred yards out, swimming back and forth
in tight circles, easing their way toward shore.
He stood up to see. They were pushing
something, first one and then the other, nosing

it up into the surf, up toward the waiting father.
Of course it was. The boy rolled toward him in the water,
Jerry waded out, and the water was cold.
That's exactly the story he told
to me, standing next to my desk,
holding his own hands. I couldn't just ask,
Well, what else happened? or, *Was the tank strapped on still?*
He stood there, staring at me, until —

I knew what he wanted from me,
so I cried. I cried enough so he could see
I cared about him. And then I sold him a car.
What do I do, close down, go to a bar
with him and get shit-faced? What would that do?
Look, I love my kids. I'm sure you love yours, too.
But that's a separate kind of intimacy.
My customers are feeding my family.

I better know their idiosyncrasies.
I can't show them who I am, but I give them me.
Me. That's right. I give me.
I become a part of their intimacy,
and some of them welcome me in, when they can.
But I listen to them, I cry, I make friends.
You want to sell, remember — you make yourself
into a virgin — you get a new thrill every time you sell.

10

On Easter, the day before my grandfather died,
I sat and sang for him, quietly —
I'll be loving you, always . . . always —
and I still say
I heard him whispering along with me,
but from someplace up above his hospital bed,
where this long shadow
slanted off toward the Venetian blinds.

The Friday after, I dreamed he rang my doorbell.
"I can name those stars in your eyes," he said.
"You're in Graceland Cemetery, Grandad . . . you're dead,
and I have a date with Paul."
He was waltzing with himself in my hallway.
"Don't tell them I can dance
when you visit," he said, bending at the waist.
"I won't get any rest at all."

11

Can't none of you say my Kevin died in some street fight.

There ain't no gun-holes Cal Johnson puttied full of make-up.

Can't none of you say this coffin lid's shut.

You look. There ain't no stitches on my boy's face.

Can't none of you say my Kevin ain't beautiful.

Even thinned out so frail, my boy still looks beautiful.

Can't none of you say how he cried being born.

He found my nipples quick and he hung on, just quiet.

Can't none of you say my boy didn't work.

We got our own paid-for house you all go by.

Can't none of you say praise Jesus for this, sister.

What you know about love?

Can't none of you say who's better off where.

Which one of you is gonna fix my heart back?

Can't none of you say what's dead is gone.

I know the words already for shut-away bones.

Can't none of you say how anything means.

Can't none of you say what wants to be.

12

Seven value dots for one large, single-topping pizza —
that was their deal. So right at 6 pm, in front of City Hall,
with the TV cameras humming, the head Domino's guy hands
sixteen large pizzas over to me, for free.

I smile, hand him back 112 value dots. They weren't free.
I dove in a lot of greasy dumpsters for those pizza
boxes with the red dots. Cut both my hands
more than once picking through. Some piss-on-the-floor hall

ain't right for my Sarah's seventh birthday, some hall
where crack-heads walk around passing out free
rides to little kids, and where some old guy's got his hands
working overtime in one of the dark corners. That pizza

fed all of us on 9th street every sausage bite of birthday pizza
we could fit. We ain't ever going back to no barracks hall
where they watch you get dressed and lay their hands
on your cot. Air, sun, water, hands, pizza. They're all free.

13

Okay, Kathy woke up at 3 A.M.,
     with a certified mega-contraction.
         "Must be false labor again,"

she groaned. "I'll be fine. Go back to sleep."
     "What, you must be crazy," I said.
         "You're eight days overdue."

By 3:30, we had consistent contractions,
     three minutes apart and counting down.
         I see knowing smiles around this circle—

we're confessing to the experienced here, honey.
     Well, Kathy was in the shower, by then, crying,
         and I was on the line with Houdini,

our midwife. You call her that, too?
     Janet Hodenius of WomanCare,
         the unrivalled baby magician.

Houdini tried to deflate my hysteria—
     "Get dressed, pack Kathy's bag, walk downstairs."—
         basic, centering stuff, like inhale/exhale.

4 A.M., news trucks nosing along curbs,
     cop cars paired up at Dunkin' Donuts,
         squirrels cracking acorns mid-avenue,

and us, zooming into the first, glorious pink
     of dawn over the Mystic River. I remember thinking,
         what a perfect day to be born.

Well, you know what happens at hospitals—
        admitting forms, fetal monitors, birthing rooms—
                nothing unusual until the tub room.

Like a stainless steel bumper car with no steering wheel,
        the tub had a side door with a gasket
                that inflated to hold all the water inside.

From the minute Kathy climbed in there,
        she was set to sign a mortgage
                on that tub. "Forever," she said,

"let me just stay in here forever.
        Wake me when it's over."
                Three hours she stayed in that tub.

"The baby will be a giant prune," I told her.
        Nada. Forget it. Wasn't about to budge.
                By 9, though, she was 7 centimeters,

and breathing hard between contractions.
        The tub room was pretty small,
                maybe eight feet square at most,

but it had a shower, too. No stall,
        just a rectangle of brown tile
                on the floor, and a white, vinyl curtain

that you pulled around on a curved track above.
        So Kathy moved to the hot shower,
                and held onto a wooden chair for a while.

But she was losing it. I could tell.
        She would clench her fists together white
                or squeeze the chair-back hard

when each contraction came on,
        bow her head and moan out
                in a rhythmic, guttural chant

that built to an elemental scream,
        and then broke down into sobbing.
                That was the hardest part for me,

to hear and see all her pain like that—
        to wipe her head with an ice-filled cloth,
                fan away the steam, open the door,

turn up the shower, close the door, whatever—
        none of it took away that pain.
                About 11, her water broke.

Houdini okayed Kathy pushing then,
        but she was almost worn out.
                Eight hours of hard labor, no drugs,

and frustration was starting to win.
        The baby's head had barely crowned.
                That's when Houdini went to work.

"You stand here and hold the railing;
        you twine your hands behind his neck;
                you lock your legs and I'll lift hers.

"Push now; here we go; that's it; again."
        God, it was worse than football drills,
                and louder than a jungle symphony.

There we were, all of us stripped down,
        in that relentless shower with billowing steam,
                in the constant screaming and straining

and me laughing in my nervous gusts
　　　　　to scare away my own fear,
　　　　　　　　　and the whole thing swallowing us so long

it seemed somehow all of us were starting over,
　　　　　that my days before then had been a dull waiting
　　　　　　　　　for that frenzied, timeless pushing.

I looked down, finally, between us,
　　　　　in a thin space that showed light
　　　　　　　　　as we all shoved down together,

and I saw the new body squirt out,
　　　　　and Houdini's hands flying under him,
　　　　　　　　　catching that eternal, slippery pass.

Then we all sank down, crying out,
　　　　　in the gigantic, magic second
　　　　　　　　　before the mechanics of suctioning began,

inside the swirl of blood and birth waters,
　　　　　and we held the umbilical rope
　　　　　　　　　strung between Kathy and our baby,

glowing in the steam like a string
　　　　　of translucent, beaded snail shells,
　　　　　　　　　blue streaked with red, leading back to ocean.

14

Look at me, mom, I'm hiding, and then,
I told you, mom, look, look at me, he yells,
burrowing down through the souvenir footballs
his father still sends,
tossing toys out to make me answer:
the musical egg-bird with cloud-shaped wings
first, the bell in its one bulbous foot warning
me to remember
something. Then a dump truck tumbles out,
half-crushed, and a red snow boot, with the word
LEFT stamped inside a diagonal blizzard
of worn-down grooves cut
into its sole. *I'm a good monster,*
he growls, *a mommy monster,* and throws
a striped cigar box, full of midget cowboys,
just to see whether
I'll ever stop him. And so I do.
I grab his arms, I squeeze, I lift him up;
holding him at arm's length, I want to scream, *Stop,*
or, *I can't stand you,*
as I pull him, slowly, to my face.
He reaches down my blouse to touch my breast,
his automatic comfort now, his dream-test
to see if I'll place
his mouth there one more time and let him suck
me even flatter, as Sesame Street
and the lost afternoons repeat, and repeat.
Give me my life back,
I do yell, too loud. His mouth will open
now, I know, into an oval of pain,
but I close my eyes, tight, and try to imagine
my own life again.

15

dear santa,

prince george hotel
number 46
near the garbage stairs
i wanna put where we live up on top here
so you know
we move again last summer
my mom always say don't answer nobody
they knock loud or yell she don't care
just stay quiet
but she say it's ok to tell you we live here
so i am
i been good an bad i'm not lying
because i know you know no matter what
when my gran die
i start to sit by her window an look
watch out for her soul
my mom say it fly off now
gran try to breathe an breathe that night
but her soul got caught
trying to flap out
i touch her to try an feel the wings
but she cough cough cough cough cough
i wrap up in all her shirts
an they smell like she smell
what i wanna tell about
is the pigeon
even if you know i wanna tell you
she stand there an watch me with her eye
she open her mouth an take in the wind
an fly fast when she wanna eat

she swoop my mom say
so i spread froot loops down an wait
sit an wait
quiet in my gran's shirts
off on one side
where she don't even see me
i got the window set up above
she don't know
till i slam the window down so fast
an she break
she look up with that same eye then
an she start to cough
so i dip her in the water pot
we boil on our hot plate
over an over
dip that head an eye in together
to bring her back
but her head just keep loose a long time
i been good too
i sweep all the floor an i kill the mice
ask my mom
what i wanna ask for is 2 things
1 is another baby tammy that drinks an wets
i know you bring me my first one
i'm sorry
her head fall off when i love her too hard
an some pills for my mom
is the other
she say they help her move the mountain
right off her back
so when you come i keep my window up all the way
open so you can see me
an i can save you my dinner
i ask my mom about elfs
an she say i can be one if you need more

if you need me i will
i work an work an work
i wanna try an see how you fly
thank you
merry xmas to you this year
an to mrs claus your wife
an all the elfs there

16

You've worked Indiana, right?
You ever been to Crawfordsville?
I ended up stuck there last November,
had a Saturday night and all of one Sunday to kill.

Long story short, got lucky, screwed
this Italian girl — no, woman —
the 90's, I forget, you know.
I drink, I get a little crude. But Christ, human's

the only harmless term these days.
Anyway, she had overalls
on, but the bib hung low, had to.
Anna. I could feel the blaze revive inside my balls

every time she laughed or leaned toward
me. Her old, blue shoulder straps
meandered up over those beauties
like bungey cords strapped over cantaloupes.

Whew, I was dying, no kidding.
Seven months on the road,
servicing accounts, no wife checking on me anymore.
I left her waiting at home three years. With a fat load

like me, of course she left — what could I expect?
Grand Rapids to Kalamazoo,
Lansing to Greencastle, Albion, Columbus,
Dayton, risking my neck every goddamn time I flew

some commuter crop-duster from this
shit-hole here to that shit-hole there.
So I was due. She stood up
and laid a hot kiss on me, tongue in my mouth, I swear.

"Where the hell are you going?" I said.
She tossed me her pocketbook,
stared back and with both hands adjusted her tits.
Then she went to the head. Hey, take a look

past those propeller blades, at that nose,
shining. "Go ahead, touch me,"
it's saying. Yeah, right, sit on a cloud
sometime, buddy. I don't remember, really,

about her clothes. I had my shirt
still on, a button or two
unhooked, and then she clamped her legs
up high, where it hurts. But she was soaking wet, so who

cares. Would you? So then, partway
through it, something happened.
She started to whimper, out of nowhere,
and pulled away. She jammed herself against the end

of the bed. Then she slammed her face with her fist.
Maybe I shouldn't have stayed.
"I'll never forget this," she said.
"I kissed a goddamn elephant. Shit, I had to get laid

by this," and she pointed at me. I think there's a sadness
in Indiana, you know.
That probably sounds stupid, now,
coming from me. I don't think less of myself. I go

wherever I want. I like my life.
I saw a photo once,
a fox trapped in a ring of townspeople
holding axe-handles, clubs. LIFE magazine. Didn't make sense

to me. There was a real husky kid, my size,
smiling, and by his feet,
two sprawled foxes. There was a cop, too,
I think. But the eyes. The eyes of that kid about to beat

that last fox. Those were Anna's eyes.
Have you got enough space?
People turn, see me looking for a seat, and
pray. I'm one of those fat guys they're afraid to face.

I took my shirt off that night, back
at my motel, and looked, to try
and tell what exactly she hated about me.
She came on to *me,* Jack. Who knows why?

17

after dad left
my sister sucked her thumb a lot
and mom hated it
you help her stop she said
big brothers are important that way
so i pulled it out and held it a long time
pretend we're trees with no wind
i told her
but it didn't work
she yelled and stuck it back in
we let boris the box turtle we found on the road
sleep overnight
in with my ninja hermit crabs
green pepper and pepperoni
but only a day because he'd die mom said
i know
i put my finger in green pepper's swirly hole
and he wouldn't let go
boris slept under a magnolia leaf
with his head pulled in
which was smart
we had a dog i kissed
and on the mouth where germs live
he bit the letter woman
so he lives with dad now in New Mexico
last week before kindergarten
my sister snuck into nanna's sun room
and crammed some leaves of a fido tree
inside her nose
the ambulance flashed down the street
then all the way up nanna's round driveway

everyone was running
i rode in back and mom cried
you can suck your thumb honey she kept saying
then they vacuumed the wet leaves out
i got two lollipops for waiting
and jesse the ambulance man came over
for some birthday cake
and not just once now either but three times already

18

They want to throw my father out now.
        Pack him up, issue a full refund,
                and keep this incident very quiet.

They already fired the nurse.
        She was 47, and he is, well, 71 next month.
                "You're as young as you kiss, honey."

He laughed after he said that to me.
        His old bathrobe was hanging open,
                and I could see his bypass scars.

One was near his heart of course,
        where you would expect the line,
                but the other was a garish stripe

that rose from over his right knee
        up into where his shorts covered.
                I had to look away from that,

so I stared out his window,
        and at that very second I looked out,
                a great blue heron lifted off

from where the home's lawn
        sloped down into a pouch of reeds.
                I must have gasped, or said, "Oh, look,"

I can't remember what I did,
        but he stood up to see.
                The heron flapped away across the river

and landed by a green canoe
        overturned on someone's lawn.
                Then my father turned, smiling,

and folded his arms around me.
        I could see my mother's picture
                still out on his nightstand,

and his smell smelled like the grass
        in our yard on Camellia Street used to.
                Then he kissed my forehead.

"A simple case of supply and demand,"
        he said. "All those beautiful widows.
                You know how I like to be liked."

19

dear nanna our tent has not one leak anywhere i checked
i have to write quietly the sun is starting to come inside
this card is so wide words can go all the way across to here
dad is still asleep with gretchen who we met last night
after she played violin for the henry play with cannons
i can hear the russian river filled up from rain outside
one thing is i miss my mom can you call and tell her that
my dad said i can't send this card but i will find a way to
these are social nudes with oranges who love the sunshine
the woman holding two oranges by the man's long penis
is smiling with sunglasses like yours with slanty corners
boy is he strong a whole washtub of oranges with one hand
don't look if dad's right you won't understand social nudes
but you saw grandpa's penis five kids that ought to hold you
he said everybody's got a body so what no more room i love you

20

I tell you, my father had some great stories.
God knows if they were true.
Well, he took care of his dad's horses,
his trotters, every day after school.

The two of them liked each other, don't get me wrong,
but my father was a typical kid.
He fell too fast asleep with Becky Lang
in the hayloft one day, both curled

up in their birthday suits on that hot afternoon,
when his old man, at least
according to my father's version,
lifted him left ear first

with a pitchfork tine straight out of the hay
and hopped him around the loft.
My dad wouldn't have stayed with farming anyway.
Earliest chance he got he left.

He never hated the village of Mechanicville —
he just dreamed about his own company.
So he rode the train to the business school
on State Street down in Albany.

He did fine all through that Fall semester,
at the end of 1913,
the last year before the First Big War.
But after Christmas vacation,

the morning school began again in January,
a sheet of frozen rain
lay on the ground. It was so slippery
milk-horses were falling down.

My dad woke that day with a bloody nose,
and he was late for the train.
He saw it leaving the station, and chased
along the tracks behind.

He got close enough to jump at the last car
but he missed, and his right foot
slid on some ice and slipped under
one of the wheels. The front

of his foot was sliced clean off. That's true.
No one who saw him walk
questioned that. Well, the guy in the caboose
saw my father leap, then fall,

and heard the scream. So they wired down to Watervliet
for an ambulance wagon,
and propped up what was left of his foot
to keep him alive. Imagine

being him, looking where you had toes before
and seeing a squared-off, open
shoe, all filled up red. The terror
of being seventeen,

and knowing then you'd never run again —
that's what turned him old
and mean in one long, stupid moment.
Maybe not. How can we tell

which one loss in our lives shaped us?
But he was mean after that,
and all through my childhood. Some days
I'd leave when school let out

and meet my mother coming up the street,
clothes half-out of her bags,
her face all puffed up raw and bloody.
I'd grab onto one of her legs —

"Don't leave, Ma," I'd start yelling,
or some baloney like that,
and she'd just drag me along with her, telling
me she'd never go back,

not ever again. But they never got divorced.
One afternoon I found him
kneeling on her shoulders, punching her face,
and I hit him with an oak limb

we were supposed to burn. Twelve stitches
it took to close him up.
My mother got to her feet, screaming, snatched
the stick and gave me a wallop.

"That's your father," she yelled. "Leave us alone."
I'll tell you how tough he was.
When they put him in that horse-drawn wagon,
they forgot to lock the doors.

He was in back alone, on a litter,
and St. Mary's Hospital
sat on top of a hill. Just before
they got there, as the horses pulled

to make the crest, the rear doors flew open
and the litter slid right out.
So there he is, half of one foot gone
and all that blood he'd lost,

he reaches up and grabs an iron bar
to keep from going down.
And his half-foot bounced as he hung there
along the icy cobblestones.

He was a tough guy. When he was dying,
after his kidneys started to bleed,
I remember looking over at him lying
in his hospital bed,

and I said, "You can't die." He couldn't hear.
He was in an oxygen tent,
all swollen and white like a human polar bear
somebody had shot and sent

down from the arctic in some crazy dream
you never think could be real.
I stood there and wanted to scream,
"You're an iron man. You're steel.

"You won't die." Maybe I said it out loud.
Maybe just to myself, inside.
But he motioned me over to his bed.
He wanted my face beside

his oxygen tent. It was just about
over then, but he strained
at his tubes and pressed his lips tight
to the plastic, for me. And I prayed.

ACKNOWLEDGMENTS

Grateful acknowledgment is made to Dave Smith and to *The Southern Review*, in which an earlier version of "The Slave Ship" appeared.

I am indebted to the Virginia Commission for the Arts for an Individual Artist Project Grant in 1993 which enabled me to finish this book.

I am grateful to many friends for helping me with their readings of these poems. W.D. Snodgrass and Norton Girault provided insightful and extensive criticisms at a crucial point in the book's development. Phil Raisor was a good friend and a supportive reader at a time when it would have helped him to abandon me. Marea Gordett helped me refine the focus of the dramatic monologues in the third section, and Dana Wildsmith extended much-needed counsel and support. David Fenza, Wayne Ude, Marian Blue, Roxanne French-Thornhill, Karen Maceira and my other friends and colleagues at the Ude-Blue writer's workshop in Norfolk suffered amiably through the early drafts of the historical narratives in Section 2, and their critical abilities pointed me in what seemed to be the right directions again and again. Thank you to all of them.

To Al Poulin, Jr., Thom Ward, and Steve Huff, my editors and friends at BOA, I extend my sincere thanks for all their invaluable suggestions. I could not have made this book without their abilities and insights.

I am most indebted to Stacey, my intimate partner, for being my first and last reader, for enduring countless readings of not only my poems, but of all my writing, and almost always responding with wisdom and discrimination, and for relentlessly dragging me with her toward the Divine, even in the years when the task appeared hopeless.

ABOUT THE AUTHOR

Born in Troy, New York, William B. Patrick is the author of *Roxa: Voices of the Culver Family* (BOA, 1989), a novel in prose and poetry which won the 1990 Great Lakes Colleges Asociation New Writers Award for the best first work of fiction, and *Letter to the Ghosts*, a book of poems published in 1977 by Ithaca House. He has also written several feature-length screenplays, plays for both stage and radio, and a teleplay, *Rachel's Dinner*, which starred Olympia Dukakis and aired nationally on ABC-TV in 1991.

Mr. Patrick has taught creative writing at Onondaga Community College, Salem State College, and Old Dominion University. He has received grants from the Academy of American Poets, the National Endowment for the Arts, the Massachusetts Artists Foundation, and the Virginia Commission for the Arts.

Most recently, having returned to his hometown, he completed eighteen months of research with the professional firefighters and paramedics in Troy, riding with them to fires, rescues, and emergency medical calls. From that experience, Mr. Patrick has written his most recent screenplay, *Fire Ground*, has shot and edited a ninety-minute video documentary titled *Saving the City*, and is currently writing *When No One Else Will*, a creative nonfiction book that follows the firefighter paramedics of the Troy Fire Department's 1st Platoon for one full year.

BOA EDITIONS, LTD.
AMERICAN POETS CONTINUUM SERIES